T0078121

Homestead Ranch

ARIKA HORNER

authorHOUSE®

AuthorHouse™
1663 Liberty Drive
Bloomington, IN 47403
www.authorhouse.com
Phone: 833-262-8899

Published by AuthorHouse 05/18/2022

ISBN: 978-1-6655-6009-2 (sc)
ISBN: 978-1-6655-6008-5 (e)

Print information available on the last page.

This book is printed on acid-free paper.

"Two roads diverged in a wood, and I—I took the one less traveled by, And that has made all the difference." – Robert Frost
"That's the only way I know
Don't stop 'til everything's gone
Straight ahead, never turn round
Don't back up, don't back down
Full throttle, wide open
You get tired and you don't show it
Dig a little deeper when you think you can't dig no more
That's the only way I know" – Jason Aldean,
featuring Luke Bryan and Eric Church

Thank you to everyone who has listened to me,
and encouraged me to reach my dreams.
Thank you to my family for making me who I am.
I couldn't do it without any of you.
Love you.

Contents

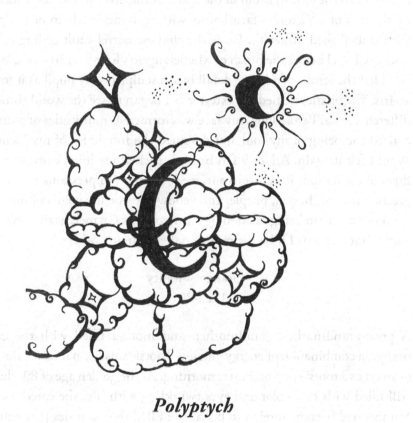

Polyptych

Self-Portrait
1998-

Every part of me is represented through a multitude of pigmentation that designs my portrait. I began as a blank canvas at birth, waiting to be filled in with color. Who I am was not known? Who I became was yet to be determined? I was the OG of a black and white sitcom that aired on Friday nights when the kids were out of the house at the drive-in movies. I was the foundation of a Victorian farmhouse, with its bones ready to be sculpted with embellished millwork. I was the shallow barrel vault ceiling of the Sistine Chapel before the brush of Michelangelo's four-year frescoes. Wait!

I felt the stroke of a No. 7 detail brush sculpting my pupil as it forms an iris. The bristles tickled my exterior as I began to see the world through different lenses. Before long, my face was formed as multitudes of painters crafted the being of my soul and designed the interludes of my identity. Wait! I felt it again. A No. 9 fan brush breached my linen canvas with a flush of coloration. It began to surface just as the impressions of orange, green, blue, red, brown, purple, and yellow became my colors of me.

For now, I am being filled in by numerous 4 x 6 panels as they become a sole. But one day, I'll be the mosaic pallet of many others.

Orange: Vitality
1922-2011

A great-grandmother, grandmother, and mother filled with the color orange, a combination of energy and joy. Tootsie was her name, for she was as sweet as a tootsie pop on Easter morning. At the golden age of 89, cheeks still filled with rosy color and eyes twinkling with life, she cared for all. Hunger had become foreign to her as she filled the tummies that entered her home. Not a discriminative bone in her body, anyone she met became an extension of her family tree. As a child, I would walk across the field to her white two-story farmhouse, excited to see the great-grandmother that was so much more. She was the canner of pears and supplier of sweets for six children, fourteen grandchildren, and thirteen great-grandchildren. To us, her energy radiated from one generation to the next. She was the mortar to the cement of our family unit that could never be mended. Tootsie, my great-grandmother, brought the vitamin c of life to my childhood, shaping the essence of my optimistic spirit.

Green: Nature and Abundance
1947-2021

Mary, quite contrary, was far from the truth. Mary, my equine grandma, made my childhood greener. My summers were filled with instructing sessions, laughs, smiles, and horsey fun. She taught me the value of nature and the trust given by the animal. She lived and breathed essence on her family farm. Born with Spina Bifida, she lived an abundant life until she was called home. Defying most expected mental and physical debilitation cases, she finished college and made it to the Para Olympics, not once but twice, as she renewed her greenery. Her supposed weaknesses became one of her biggest strengths as she lived past the thirty-year life expectancy.

In childhood, I watched a four-foot uneven legged woman guide me through the obstacles of taming the beast. I learned to sit in the saddle with my boobs to the sky and straight lines from shoulder, hip to heel, while my elbows remained by my side. At times, I found it tedious. However, I thought if Mary could do it, I definitely could. Her desire to live in the abundance of her dreams encouraged me to achieve mine. I would watch her, thinking, wow, she doesn't live at her limits. Is that the person I want to be in my adult life? Looking back through those memories, I remember she is the essence of my dreamer's attitude.

Blue: Sadness
1974-2021

At 47, a godfather passed. He had diabetes due to a poor diet and a lack of insulin to fuel his cells. For many years, doctors suggested he go on insulin so that sugars could move into his body tissues. But, like any semi-truck driver, he couldn't keep his job and be on insulin. All he knew was driving a big rig, and it was taken from him. I remember smiles and many game nights playing phase 10 where he couldn't get past the fourth phase. One night, he was stuck on it for thirteen rounds. Luck was not on his side that night. That's the Jeff I remember. The one who enjoyed his trucks, guns, knives, game nights, and popsicles on a hot summer's day.

But that wouldn't last forever. He would go on insulin because he was promised to have a job within the company outside of being a truck driver. Sadly, they lied to him. As soon as he went on it, he was fired. Because of their sleaze bag ways, I watched the happy Jeff turn into a shell of who he was. He was engulfed by the blue rain of Zeus's tears. Through his short life, I learned that life could be altered at any moment. The job I have may not be guaranteed forty years from now. Promises of others are just words until their actions are decided. My godfather, Jeff, taught me to live every day as my last because it may be my last.

Red: Love and Passion
1948-2022

Elizabeth, otherwise called Lizzy, emanated the Root chakra of red. Her love and passion for her family could meet no others. She was there when Tootsie could no longer live on her own. She was there when her children needed her. She was there to put smiles on the faces of her grandchildren. She was there when I managed to get stuck underneath the dining room table as I reached for a piece of candy.

"Help Lizzy, I'm Stuck," I shouted as she zoomed over in her scooter from the kitchen sink, laughing at my foolishness.

My great aunt, who was, by all means, my grandmother, never failed to show her Muladhara love. We spent nights baking and decorating cookies for Halloween and Christmas. She taught me how to wrap presents, stitch fabric, and change my academic trajectory by offering a dollar for every A I earned. Without her, I wonder if I would be at the academic level I am. She pushed me to display the same amount of love and passion she had towards others in my life. Every day, I miss her smiles and the red warmth exuding from her figure as the longest wavelength. Like the red room in Tootsie's farmhouse, she was my home. Lizzy, the naked red rose, crafted the contents of my heart.

Brown: Dependability
1971-

Brown, primarily viewed as a dull, dingy color, bears more stability than any other member of the color wheel. For me, dad was and still is an everyday presence. Whether in person or in spirit, the lessons from my childhood still ring true. No matter what activity my sister and I did with him, he taught us to give it a hundred and ten percent. He strives for perfection and insists on maximum effort. Growing up, he would always say, "Why do it twice if you can do it right the first time." I grew up with it engrained in my mind and still think about it whenever I'm completing homework or activities in my daily life.

So, my father, who exhibits the rare representation of oak, is responsible for the work ethic that drives me each day. He is an essential part of my life. He's the father that's always one call away at any time of day or night. The father that I can't live without. Its most often said that little girls depend on their fathers. For me, it's a reality. My father, the brown earth, is responsible for the drive that pushes me always to be a better version of myself than the day before.

Purple: Creativity
1954-

The art of illustration is represented through Susan, otherwise known as Gma. Like a hummingbird, which happens to be her favorite bird, her spirit is filled with joy and light. My right cerebral hemisphere thinking Gma transferred her thinking to me. Like her, I think in lines of poetry filled with purple that awakens my senses. I would spend nights with her as she wrote in the most beautiful calligraphy and painted pictures of animals. Last Christmas, she painted a picture of my sister's dog. It looked so realistic that I thought it would jump off the canvas.

When I think about those times, I remember wanting to be able to do that too. Somehow, I have found a way to be semi-close to her talents. Her influence pushes me to think outside the box about what should or shouldn't be considered creative. Through her, I learned art is represented through the color purple as it aligns with the universe. It has no limits and cannot be boxed in by standards and regulations. She is free to be herself even if the right side is anomalous as lilacs in nature. Like my father's Pink Grandma, she is my purple Gma, who is responsible for the tastefully decadent original side of me.

Present Yellow: Happiness in Sisterhood
1998-
2000-

Unity between siblings, related through blood or friendship, demonstrates the deeper meaning of family. The blood creates genetic ties, while sisterhood brings an addition to my family unit. Janell, A.K.A. bird or nelly, portrays the blood side of sisterhood, while Autumn, A.K.A. sis, demonstrates family not by blood. Their combination creates a yin and yang balance between genetics and relationship. We grew up with each other. Our parents were friends, and so were we. To us, blood meant and still means nothing. We laughed, played, and found happiness and comfort in each other's presence. Even though we have started our journeys in life, our relationship will always be there.

For us, time is non-existent. The high-energy happiness in our childhood brought years of yellow that appeared as if time had not passed since we got together. The influence of my sisters reminds me to have joy and incorporate the increased metabolism of yellow into my life. Bird-Sis is the perfect combination of laughter, smiles, happiness, giggles, and sunshine. They created the laughter that finds me when life gets in the way. Bird-Sis is and will always be why I laugh through trials and tribulations. Because of the lemon heads, I will never remain beaten.

Identity: Colors of Me

What does this all mean? Well, to me, each color is essential. Color symbolism and perception are the base of my infrastructure and framework. While some parts may be in the past or present of life, the make-up of my bones does not recognize time. Each shingle has been passed through many phases. Tootsie passed her lessons to Lizzy. Lizzy gave her lessons to me, and I will pass them to my children. The beam of every individual becomes the circle of life. Our influences become the influences of others, whether we realize it or not.

The representation of our world is one interconnected farmhouse. Our energy and values bounce off each other as sound waves bounce off my walls. So, to find out who I am, I had to reflect on my polyptych (a painting made of multiple panels). Even though society tries to fit each of us into a mold, we have the power to create our color wheel that is a representation of our experiences and interactions with influential individuals in our lives. By discovering my color wheel, I have found the good and bad moments, but I choose to see the positivity in the good and learn from the unfavorable.

Impact: Farmhouse Legacy

Now, I must choose the impact I want to leave behind me. As I pass on my colors to others, I will decide to put my mark on the world through existing. While I will continue to feel brushstrokes paint my walls, the colors of me will radiate to those who need a helping hand or a moment of reprieve. Inspiration will be more than just a thought. The impact will be more than just a word in my dictionary. As I sit rooted in my storm cellar, waiting to welcome additions to my self-portrait, the effect will become a virtue in my life. I am no longer just the framework of my house. I have graduated to a two-story five-bedroom two-bath centennial farmhouse.

I will be the hundred old legacies that transcend the grasp of time and continue through generations. My gift will be that of the white farmhouse of my youth with green shutters, filled with painters and sculptors, transforming my walls as the mosaic of my farmhouse remains.

Chapter 1

 ## "Mamma's Place"

Whiteboards, lines, graphs, charts, and terms that mean nothing to me, run across the projector screen, as Mrs. Wilder scribbles on the foils with her black ink. Mrs. Wilder is a sweet teacher, frail and nimble in her movements. Wearing thick-framed glasses, held around her neck with a pearl chain, she has eyes that can pierce your soul, while her lessons numb your brain. I'm in the accelerated business program at my high school, and Mrs. Wilder teaches the accounting portion of it. While I love her as a person, I hate this program and can't wait to get home to the family farm.

My great grandfather started the farm when he was a young man. We have pictures of him in our family photo album, as a brazen, strong, and lively young fellow. Every Sunday he attended church, where he met my great grandmother. She was an eyecatcher, as he would say. She loved farm life and her animals, especially her horses. Her golden honey brown hair gleamed under the sun and her smoldering brown eyes you could get lost in. As he watched and admired her sturdy yet flexible figure, which allowed her to perform rodeo tricks effortlessly on her stallion, my great grandfather as the legend goes, took one glance at her and was "smitten like a kitten." My father says he was placed under her love spell, and only had eyes for her.

Sometimes, I try to picture what Salyersville, Kentucky, looked like in the time of my great grandfather. Most of the older buildings and general stores have been morphed into a city-like town. I've always wondered what the town and family life looked like. My family tells me I have an old soul. I like to think I was born into the wrong generation. My father has never understood my love for country life, as he continuously pushes me to get better grades to qualify for a free ride to college. I don't understand why he pushes me so hard to get away from the farm and see big cities. It makes me wonder if he is happy with his family legacy.

"Victoria," Mrs. Wilder says sternly, trying to hide her amiability with annoyance.

"Yes," I reply, breaking from my internal thoughts.

"Would you mind paying attention to the lesson? You don't get to doze off in class," she says as she musters an authoritative teacher-like face.

"Yes Mrs. Wilder," I reply. She is a sweet lady but always demands respect from students during her classes.

I grab my pencil and scribble meaningless charts and accounts on my notepad. In just a single class period, she always draws and writes so many notes and charts, my notebook is reaching capacity.

As the class period drags on, my hand grows tired and begins to cramp at the speed of note-taking.

The sound of the bell releases me from the blockade of learning.

Letting out a sigh of relief, I zip my bag closed and sling it over my shoulder. Walking through the hallways, I grab my phone, checking for a list of chores from my father. Every day he sends one for my sister and me. Before I can complete them today, I have a shift at "Mamma's Place," the local diner in town. The owner is a friend of my mother, who goes by Mrs. Kay. She has known us as far back as I can remember. Last summer, she gave me a job at the dinner.

Snapping my phone shut, I'm stopped by my classmate Sky as I reach the doors. She is a spunky redhead with green eyes who sits next to me in accounting. She usually borrows my notes, since she is not as focused as I am during class.

"Hey!" she exclaims in her squeaky voice.

Chuckling, "I'm guessing you want to borrow my notes?"

"Yeah! If you wouldn't mind. I was also wondering if you were okay after last week's fight with Billy. I've got to say you're usually a calm person, but those boys brought a different side of you out," she says, looking at me with concern.

"I hate Billy because he is always hitting on me. It started in seventh grade when he decided to corner me one day under the bleachers. When he tried to make a move, I gave him a black eye. Ever since that day, he won't leave me alone no matter what I do to him." I shift my weight from one foot to the other as the corners of her mouth drawdown and her eyes dilate.

"That would make any girl angry. Thanks for the notes!" She says as she turns towards her locker.

"Welcome," I holler back as I fish my truck keys out of my pocket and walk out to the parking lot.

I drive a midnight purple 2010 Ford Ranger with, five-speed manual transmission. There's no sign of rust anywhere on it. The purple is rich and dark as the midnight sky. Along the sides of the body, a herd of galloping mustangs runs from the tailgate to the bumper. Inside, waterproof purple seat covers protect the hand-stitched and embroidered charcoal black leather seats. The dashboard is simple and clean with its gages, air vents, stereo, charging port, and heating and air-conditioning controls. The truck is one of the few possessions I have of his.

While my grandfather loved continuing the family farm, his second love was building trucks in his free time. He built this one and gave it to me on my sixteenth birthday. A couple of years ago, he passed away from a sudden heart attack. Every time I look at it, I remember his big grin and the twinkle of excitement in his eyes when he worked on vehicles.

Extending my arm, I open the door and toss my bag into the passenger seat. Placing the key in the ignition, the engine turns over. Mamma's Place isn't far from the school. It's within walking distance, but I won't leave my truck here.

Passing through town, I round the street corners until Mamma's Place is insight. It's the one building that has kept its rustic appearance. Mrs. Kay loves the agrestic look and refuses to change it. It's why I love working for her. Every shift is a blast to the past, providing me a sense of proximity to grandpa's story. Today, I am only working for a couple of hours, as one of the waitresses called in sick the other day and I told her I would fill in for a little bit.

Before I can get through the door, a body pushes me backward.

"I'm so glad you're here!" Mrs. Kay exclaims.

"I haven't had that big of a greeting in a while. What brought it on?" I ask.

"Nothing, just happy to see you," she replies with a smirk on her face.

"Like hell, I'm going to believe that. Tell me what's going on," I say. I can always tell when she is lying. She gets this big grin like she is going to fall on the floor laughing.

"Oh, fine you caught me," she grumbles with annoyance at being caught. "I heard the nuisance clan was going to come by here and cause some trouble. I am hoping you would chase them out of the diner."

"Sure thing, Mrs. Kay. I hate those boys always thinking they have the run of the town," I assure her. Those boys have always aggravated me. TDuring the day, they terrorize the town. At night they run the hayfields, tearing up the soil and crops. The farmers have to keep watch at night, protecting their fields from lifted trucks performing donuts. Luckily my family raises cattle, so we don't have to worry about fields. We only had one run-in with them when I was younger and they tried to cut the fences. They were electrocuted before they could finish the job.

I owe it to her for the support she has given me in my writing. She is always pushing me to tell my father.

Hanging my jacket in the backroom, I grab my apron and secure it around my hips. I begin my shift waiting on the regulars, starting with Mrs. Jenkins the owner of the flower shop. She comes to pick up her usual turkey and rye sub for lunch. Her hair is chocolate brown and filled with little florets. Her eyes are a golden hazel that light up when she smiles. She wears blue jeans, rhinestone boots, a floral shirt, and her apron every day. I enjoy how she always gives me a big hug when she gets her lunch.

When I walk over to Mr. Wilson, he is fidgeting with his black-rimmed spectacles that never stay on.

"Hi, there dear! Can I have my usual cup of tomato soup and grilled cheese?" he asks with a big grin. He works at the bank as a teller and wears a blue suit with black Oxfords every day. For almost a year, he sits on the middle stool at the counter as a reminder of his late wife. Her name was Mary, but she passed away from cancer last spring.

Suddenly, the door slams open, revealing the nuisance clan as they almost rip it off its hinges. Out of the corner of my eye, I catch Mrs. Kay walking out from the back and then freezing in place. "What do you want boys?" I ask with a forceful tone.

"We just want some dinner and maybe some company tonight," the oldest, Willy, says with a suggestive raise of his bushy, untrimmed eyebrows.

"You pay for your food, but you aren't getting any company from me tonight or any night, for that matter," I snap back at him, infuriated by his presence.

Billy, the youngest, reaches his grubby, tarnished hand towards me. "Well, aren't you just a cup of sunshine? Do you want us to cause a problem here?"

Seeing my chance to get rid of them, I pull the right side of my shirt up, just enough to flash my Colt .45 Revolver. "Listen here, you're going to leave here, and if I see you here again this bullet is entering your body. You don't dare to grab a woman or try to lay a hand on me. NOW LEAVE," I shout in a dark menacing tone. Shifting my shirt back down, I return to my normal stance, as Billy runs out the door, with Willy and Phil following his lead.

"Thank god you were here!" Mrs. Kay pipes in from behind the kitchen doors as she walks through them.

"Were you hiding or just observing from the background?" I ask Mrs. Kay, placing my hand on my hips.

"You know I'm not one to take action," she says with a relieved smile. She has been attacked in the past and can't fight worth a lick, so I take care of her.

Mrs. Kay Flashback

Watching through a sliver of light in the closet door, I tuck my knees to my chest as I hear my boyfriend smashing beer and liquor bottles against the walls. I can hear his footsteps prowl down the hallway as he nears the bedroom.

"You think you're good enough to be a writer? Let's see," he says as he picks up my journal from the nightstand to read from it.

"Beauty . . . always judged, always said to be in the eye of the beholder. But not ever so, appearance said to be of highest importance. First impressions at every turn, A swan most pretty, but A toad most regretful. Wait!" he pauses to take a swig of Jack Daniels whiskey.

"Have the tables turned? Once pretty, now deceitful. Once regretful, now

honest. Here we are, where heads meet. Beauty, once defined. Now painted with ambiguity. Who decides?"

For a moment, silence takes over. I reach out and slide one of the doors open. I stick my head out, feeling relief when I don't see him.

"Interesting last line," he stammers. "I'll decide if you're beautiful." He grabs my hair, ripping me backward.

I tremble and cower as he repeatedly punches and kicks me. I can feel my bones crack and muscles groan in pain as he continues to knock the air out of my lungs. It goes on for what seems like hours before my eyes swell shut and darkness encloses my mind.

"Yeah, yeah," I reply, rolling my eyes, knowing all too well she can't give a beating. "I'm just glad they are gone. They better not come here anymore."

"They won't darling, you scared the living shit out of them," she assures me. "Out of curiosity, where did that pistol come from? You're only seventeen until July?" she asks with a worried look.

"My father gave it to me. He knows the trouble I have with Billy. I try not to flash it, but I don't trust him. I flip when he comes around," I inform her as I look at the counter.

"Just don't get caught, dear. I know you were taught responsibility with those, but you don't know what can happen," she says as she makes a new pot of coffee.

Gabbing a rag, I wipe the counter as I look around at the faces of the customers. They all know my father and his love of guns, so they don't pay any attention to the disturbance. Sadly, the townspeople have become used to the nuisance clan. Their father is the Sheriff and lets them run wild.

Sighing, I reach above my head and flip on the radio. As I turn the dial, the radio kicks in: **New Haven is looking for young aspiring authors. Apply now, you may get a full-ride scholarship. Show us your talent. You're just one submission away from getting everything you have ever dreamed of.**

Mrs. Kay says, "You should apply and I'm not just saying that because I think of you as a daughter. You have a great talent that should be shared with the world. Take a chance. There's nothing to lose."

I've never thought of myself as talented at combining words on paper. It's just a pastime of mine, something to clear my head and unscramble my thoughts.

Victoria's Flashback

"What are you doing?" Summer asks.

"Nothing. Be quiet before he hears you," I hush Summer.

We're in Mr. Wickham's English class. He is droning on about the requirements for our next paper.

"What is keeping your attention from my instructions?" Mr. Wickham asks.

Looking up from my notebook, "Nothing. I was just taking notes," I reply anxiously.

With an annoyed look, he walks back to the front of the class and continues with his boring instructions. I will have to remember to kick Summer for almost getting me caught. Returning my pencil to the parchment, I continue to write...

*Bent and winding, twisting and turning, my framework of fibers provides a home. I was a sapling, but no more will I sprout. No, I am **tall**, reaching towards the heavens as if I had no endpoint. Shivers run down my spine, I'm always a jungle gym or a playground for the little muskrats. Wait! I'm so much more than a mat. I'm a scenic view. I'm the source of your warmth. I'm the base and foundation of your residence. I'm the filter to your air. I'm everything while being nothing at **all**. Maybe, you'll notice me, standing **tall** or not at **all**. For now, I'm the jungle gym, but one day, I'll have it **all**.*

"I don't know, what if I'm not good enough for them?" I've always been scared of sharing my writing. I don't want people ruining my way of escape to another realm.

"Nonsense, you're amazing. Just promise me you will think about it," she begs and pleads with a look I could never say no to. She always uses her adorable puppy face to get her way.

"Okay," I agree, laughing at her persuasion method. Shaking my head, I walk over to clear Mrs. Gerber's half-eaten meal. My nickname for her is the sampler because she never finishes her plates. She likes to take half of it home for snacks.

Placing her beautifully wrinkled hand on mine, Mrs. Gerber looks at me, "You know she is right."

"You really think so?"

"I know so. Everyone does. Listen to Mrs. Kay, she knows what she is talking about," Mrs. Gerber reassures me, giving my hand a gentle squeeze of encouragement. Thanking her, I turn to take the dishes to the back and begin packaging her leftovers. What would Mrs. Kay know about writing? I wonder if she has a secret pastime. All well, maybe she is right. What would it hurt? I don't have anything to lose. Maybe my father would support the idea and get rid of his big-city dreams for me.

"It's time for you to leave, my dear," Mrs. Kay breaks through my thoughts as she hands me my belongings. Thanking her, I place my apron back in its cubby and hand Mrs. Gerber her to-go bag. Pushing the doors open, I head toward my truck. Mrs. Kay even painted my own parking space neon green for me. Smiling to myself, I open my door and slide in, starting my engine.

I look in my driver's mirror to back up, noticing it's shattered. The glass has formed a spiderweb pattern. Taped to the broken glass is a note:

> You'll be mine someday.
> Just wait and see
> -Billy

Why can't he just leave me alone? Crumpling the note into a small wad, I throw it to the floor and put my truck in reverse. I clutch the steering wheel causing my knuckles to turn white as I pull out of the parking lot.

As I drive through town, a buzzing sensation runs up my legs from the vibrations of the motor, causing my stomach to do circles as it travels down my arms. I can feel the adrenaline enter my fingertips while they drum their own melody on the steering wheel. I've always loved manuals.

Hearing the engine run and watching the RPMs rise and fall with speed is music to my ears. My father constantly says knowing how to drive a manual transmission is an important skill. He never explains why, but I don't care. I wouldn't drive an automatic anyway, they aren't any fun.

The timber pasture fences enter my sight as I reach the drive. They line the sides of the road all along the property line. My great grandfather named it Homestead Ranch. When he started it, there was only a house and barn. As generations came and years passed on, it grew to hundreds of acres with multiple barns, fields, cattle, and horses. The entrance sign hasn't changed. A simple wood board painted white with black lettering, hanging on the left side of the gate. While it has been repainted through the years, it has withstood the outdoors and remains a symbol of the early days.

Driving up my long, gravel driveway, I see my father, checking the fence lines. He checks them every day, making sure there are no breaks in the wire, so the cattle and horses can't escape. I park my truck and head off toward the barn to complete my chores.

Chapter 2

 *Sisterly Bond*

*P*ulling my phone out of my pocket, I check the time. It's six o'clock. Time to wash up for dinner. Ma always has it ready by seven. She insists on everyone eating as a family and cooks like she is feeding an army. There are lots of leftovers for lunch the next day.

Looking at the wheelbarrow full of manure, I wonder how I'm going to move it to the sizing compost bin. I don't like making a hundred trips, so I pack it as full as I possibly can. Sometimes, I load it a little too full and then struggle to move it. Eventually, I get it to the pile with a little elbow grease from my sister.

"Did you do it again?" my sister, Alexandrea, hollers behind me.

"Yes, get your ass over here and help me," I yell at her.

"Alright," she says as her eyes roll, "don't be so sassy."

Laughing at her snarky response, we grab the wooden handles and dump it. There are a few moments where it almost dumps as it hits divets in the uneven ground. Luckily, we are able to stabilize the wheelbarrow and make it to the structure.

"I don't know why you always make it so heavy," she replies.

"I'm lazy, you know that. Don't pretend you haven't known me my whole life," I smile at her as we flip the wheelbarrow over and dispose of its unpleasant contents.

"Did you hear about that scholarship offer?" she says.

"Yes, I heard it at the diner when the nuisance clan came in."

"Them again. What did you do this time?" She says as we head back towards the barn.

"I flashed my pistol at Billy. They ran away like scared little puppies

11

with their tails tucked between their legs," I say as we place the wheelbarrow back by the muckrakes along the back wall of the barn

She laughs at me, "Really, that's just as bad as when you broke Willy's wrist in middle school. He had to wear a pink cast for a week."

"And all the girls laughed at him till he turned pink like his cast," remembering their faces becoming red like a tomato.

Turning away from the wall, we head back up towards the house.

"Girlsssssssssssssssss," Ma yells from the porch, "Dinner's almost done. Get washed up."

"Coming," we yell in unison as we race the rest of the way to the house

"First one there gets the last piece of triple chocolate fudge cake for dessert!" My sister yells.

"You're on. I already claimed that yesterday." I smile at her, waiting for her to take off.

"Too bad!" She darts off towards the house. Not wanting to share the cake, I run after her, leaving a trail of dust behind me.

"Eat my dust," I holler as I pass her, reaching the front doors.

"You suck, monkey butt!" she hollers back in defeat.

"We'll see about that. Keep your eyes open while you sleep tonight," I threaten her.

Laughing, my sister nudges my arm. "You better watch out tonight," she whispers in my ear, so Ma doesn't hear our bickering.

"You girls, if it's the cake you're squabbling over. I swear you are bottomless pits," Ma scowls at our fighting.

"Oh, I will," I reply as I push past her, reaching the bathroom first. Shutting the door, I grab the handmade lavender soap from the counter that Ma always makes. She says her great-grandmother taught her when she was a child, so she tried teaching my sister and me when we were younger. I caught on quickly, but my sister was a different story. Alexandrea has always been a tomboy, managing to make a mess out of anything and everything she touches.

In the mirror, I catch my reflection. Unlike my sister's dark hair and eyes, mine is a golden honey brown. We both have the sun-kissed skin color from the Kentucky sun. Everyone always tells me I'm beautiful, even gorgeous, but I don't see what they see.

"Hurry up," my sister hollers.

"I'm done," I open the door, sliding past her grumbling, impatient form.

"Took ya long enough, now my dinner will be cold," she belly aches at me.

"You'll be fine, Ma always keeps it warm," I say as she slams the heavy, wooden door shut. The walls in the hallway are lined with floral wallpaper and a dark chocolate brown wooden trim. Mamma has family photos placed in an organized manner on them. Each photo shows the generations of my fathers' family that have lived here. In them, there is at least one son to carry out the family legacy and name. Sometimes, I feel my father's Disappointment as he stares at every photo, hoping he could've had a son. It makes me feel sad to know he can't see how much I want to stay here, take over the farm, and write our family history.

Alexandrea POV

Shutting the bathroom door, I turn and look into the mirror. As I stare at my face, a part of me wishes life was just a little bit easier for my sister and me. We always feel stressed by dad's expectations. It's hard growing up in a home where you never feel good enough. I can see it on my sister's face most of the time. She never stops studying. There are times when I wonder if the accomplishments are worth the stress.

When I look at her, I admire her for the dedication and strength she shows. I wish I could be like that someday. I want to be a daughter my parents are proud of. I want to make them happy, but I am not willing to sacrifice my happiness for theirs.

Taking one last glance in the mirror, I turn the faucet on and wash my hands. After drying them, I turn the knob and exit the bathroom, ready for dinner.

I descend the intricately carved mahogany staircase, encoded with years of fingerprints of passing generations. Unlike older staircases, mine doesn't creak as weight is placed on it. My great grandfather made it the focal point of the house. He loved carvings and moldings, so he made sure not a single detail was left out. I run my hand down the smooth intricate railing, feeling its cool touch. Then I catch a savory whiff of tonight's dinner. It's filled with the aroma of peppercorn steak, roasted potatoes, candied carrots, and Cajun fried corn. The delicious aroma lures me to the dinner table.

"That smells amazing, ma," my sister says as she takes her place across from me at the dinner table.

"Don't take any until your father gets here," Ma sayss as she sits in her chair at the end of the table. I turn my head towards the front door as I hear the clambering of boots on the steps. As it swings open, my father walks in and places his hat on the hook.

"Dinner smells good, darling," he says at my mother as he slips his boots off, placing them on the boot rack.

"Thank you, dear," Ma replies as he takes his place at the head of the table. The main course fills the center, so my father can slice it. We pass around the side dishes that sit around the main course.

"How was everyone's day?" Ma asks as we dish out food and pass around sides.

"It was normal. Just school, work, and chores like always," I reply as I scoop candied carrots onto my plate.

"Good, your teacher called me, saying you dozed off in class," my father says before he chews his steak.

"I just zoned out a little too much looking at the projector screen." I shrug my shoulders as I stuff my mouth with Cajun fried corn.

"Don't let it happen again. Remember our plan." He looks at me as he grabs some roasted potatoes.

"I know daddy. I haven't forgotten," I say, not wanting to talk about it anymore.

"Markus' Don't be so hard on her. You know how hard she works," Ma says.

"I'm sorry, Vic, I just want what's best for both of you." His usually relaxed jaw turns into a rigid line as he takes another bite of meat.

Sliding my chair back, I walk to my father's side. I turn my head to my sister, pleading for her to follow my actions as I place my hand over my father's.

"We know how much you love us, daddy. We always will remember when we were little and sat on the porch swing with you, watching the sunrise over the farm entrance." I try to reassure him.

"Yes, one of you on each side of me, sipping your morning juice as I drank my black coffee," he smiles, remembering that moment.

"We wanted some, so you gave us a sip," I smile at him.

"It was so bitter, we gagged," my sister chimes in.

My dad lifts his head, loosening his rigid jawline. As his facial muscles soften, he says, "Both of you spit it out."

"What did you tell us?" I ask him.

"Life is like coffee. Sometimes bitter, sometimes sweet. If you fall to the bitterness, hold your heart up and move towards the sweetness," he recites, breathing in deep with his eyes closed.

"Trust us, daddy. Trust how you raised us and the words you told us. We listened to every word you uttered. We will make you proud," I say. Giving him a reassuring smile, I squeeze his hand, still bigger than mine, letting him know the sincerity of my words.

"Alright, girls, you've made your old man blush. Go on up and get some rest. I'll help your mamma clean up," he says as he starts clearing plates.

"Thanks, daddio! Can we take dessert with us?" my sister pleads with her puppy eyes.

"You know I can't resist that look. Go on. Make sure you don't make a mess, and bring the plates down when you're done," he says as he walks to the kitchen.

"Sweet," we holler in unison as we grab our cake and ascend the stairs like swift birds.

Fathers Flashback

"Do you remember how to use it?" I ask my daughter, Veronica, as she points the gun at the target.

"Yep," she replies as she gets into her shooting stance.

She stands with her feet offset. Her arms are held at her shoulder height.

She leans her left cheek against her shoulder blade with her weight balanced as her hands grip the gun. Her posture screams strength as she stands grounded, ready to hit the bull's eye.

Most parents wouldn't encourage their children to shoot guns. However, I want my daughters to for protection. They are strong and spirited girls, but the world is a dark place. One day they will experience it. I want them to be prepared if something happens, especially with boys like Billy.

Standing to the side of her, I watch her inhale as she prepares to pull the trigger. Her finger slowly slides towards it as she takes in a final breath. Hearing the sharp bang of the gun, a feeling of relief washes over me. I take comfort in her new skills, as the bullet pierces the bullseye.

♊

As I open my bedroom door, I flip on the light switch and sit on my bed. It's much more comfortable than my desk chair. The comforter is as soft as a cloud, caressing every part of my body, providing the perfect amount of comfort.

Alexandrea grabs my office chair and settles into it as she asks, with a raised eyebrow, "Can I read your writing?"

"How do you know I'm writing something?" I say.

"You didn't have to. All you had to do was say you were zoning out in class," she replies as she stuffs a bite of cake into her mouth.

"That doesn't mean I'm writing something," I reply, taking another bite of cake.

"Hell, yeah it does. Don't you think I know you better than anyone?" she smiles, piling the last bit of cake off her plate into her mouth.

"Alright, if you must know. I am," I reply, shrugging my shoulders. I wait for her to ask for it.

"So, let me see it," she says, reaching her hand towards me.

Reluctantly, I reach under my pillow and hand her my notebook. On the front, I wrote the title *A Harrison Family History*.

"You wrote about us?" she asks.

"Yeah, I thought dad might like it, and I love the history here and our family legacy," I say.

Smiling, she opens the cover and starts looking at my words. As she reads, I shovel Ma's delicious cake into my mouth, inviting the warm and satisfying food to envelope my body.

Suddenly, I hear the hardcover of my notebook snap shut.

"So, is it as bad as I think it is?" I ask as I look at her frozen face.

"I…... I can't find the words to describe it," she stammers.

"So not good," I reply, looking down at my folded hands, twiddling my fingers back and forth.

"No, it's so good I don't know how to tell you how good it is," she says.

"Thanks, sis," I reply, happy she enjoyed it. However, I still have an uneasy feeling about my father.

For a moment, she stares at me, studying my face. Her eyes take in my furrowed expressions.

"Listen to me. It doesn't matter what the world thinks or even dad. You have to believe in yourself. I know you're older than me, but sometimes I can be right. You have an amazing talent that I wouldn't even dare try to match or understand. You have to use it. You can't let it waste away. Do something you love to do before you regret it for the rest of your life," she climbs off my bed grabbing my laptop from its place on my desk. "Here. Fill out the application to New Haven before you chicken out. Don't worry about dad; he will understand once you tell him how you feel and show him your talent." Alexandrea sets my laptop on my lap.

Looking at her, grateful for the bond we share, I throw my arms around her neck. "How can a baby sister be so wise?" I ask.

"Well, I get to watch all your mistakes," she mocks me.

Smiling at her reply, I say, "I couldn't imagine any better sister than you."

"You're welcome. When you tell dad tomorrow, I'll tell him that I don't want to go to college," she bargains with me.

Raising my eyebrows, I say, "So we have a deal. I will apply tonight and tell dad if you tell him with me."

"Deal," she exclaims with a triumphant smile. Climbing off the bed, she opens the door. "Goodnight, don't chicken out!" she hollers on her way to her room.

"Goodnight. I won't!" I yell back. Opening my laptop, I go to the application and begin typing a poem sample in the textbox. . .

Why can't I fly?
Why not I?
Leaves float in the
Breeze,
Grains of sand drift
In the tides,
Eagles soar above
Canyons,
Why not I?
Am I too grounded?
Does gravity have
An ironclad
Grasp on my ankles?
Are my dreams
Exceeding earth's atmosphere?
While I'm stuck,
Struggling with the
Quicksand,
Threatening to pull
Me below its surface,
Staring up at a
Dream, that's
Beyond a finger
Tips reach. . .

Chapter 3

 **Breaking Free**

"BUZZZZZZZZZZZZ," My alarm clock drones on until I slide my phone screen to turn it off. Ripping my eyes open from the dust of the sandman, I push myself into a sitting position. I hate waking up in the morning. I'm extremely slow at it. Ma always tells me I'm not a morning person, and I've always agreed with her on that. As usual, Ma's almost always right. Throwing my covers off, I feel the metal of my laptop under my hand. Smiling, I remember the events of last night.

I can't believe Alexandrea made me fill out the application, and she is going to tell dad she doesn't want to go to college. Maybe he will blow a cap. Maybe he won't. Oh well, it doesn't matter. We made a deal and it's time to do what we want with our lives. Grabbing my laptop, I swing my legs over the bed, placing my computer on the desk. Today is Saturday, so no school, but there are still chores to do. I grab a pair of wrangler jeans, a blue navy tank top, and a gray plaid short-sleeve button-down.

"You up," my sister comes in.

"Yeah," I reply. "Can you French braid my hair please?"

"Yep, if you do mine," she negotiates with me.

"Of course, isn't that what sisters are for?" I sit on the floor in front of my bed, while she sits on the bed braiding my hair. "Are you nervous?" I ask as I fidget with my hands.

"A little bit, but dad always understands and loves us. We just haven't told him what we want." She intertwines locks of my hair in and out of each other with rhythmic movements.

"I know, just nervous about what he will say," I say, feeling the butterflies rush up to my gut, making my stomach lurch in small movements.

21

"Me too but it will be okay," she says as she continues to braid my hair.

"Alright," I respond, trying to put my jitters aside. I could sit here all day while she does this. Since our mother braided our hair when we were young, I have always loved the feeling of fingers running through it. calming and almost therapeutic in nature.

"All done my turn," she says.

"Alright, switch me," I laugh as I get off the floor and sit on the bed, still warm from her bum.

Running the brush through her silky-smooth hair, I separate it into three equal chunks. Intertwining and folding the locks until they become one, I lose myself into the pattern of braiding.

"Hair tie," I say, once the last braid is completed. She hands me a black hairband. Tying up the braids, I push on her shoulders, "Let's go." After climbing down the staircase, we slip on our boots at the front door. "I'm going to do some trick riding after chores," I tell her, wanting to release my nerves.

"Sweet! Let's get them done and have some fun," she replies as she turns the front doorknob.

Shaking my head and grinning, I follow behind her as we walk to the barn to start our chores. From eight a.m. to three in the afternoon we muck stalls, feed and water the animals, mend fencing, stack hay bales from the trailer so more can be bailed, and check the horses and cattle. I'm glad I didn't just wear my tank top today because the sun would have fried my shoulders. It's shining bright this morning, creating a dry heat. Throughout the day, we push through our tasks, falling into an assembly line of rhythmic movements, causing the hours to pass by with ease.

Grabbing the green twin, I throw the last bale into the hayloft. I climb down the metal ladder and walk to Maverick's stall where I grab her apple green halter. Maverick is my 17-year-old mare trick horse.

Approaching the paddock, I unlock the gate. I can see her figure all the way in the back of the field. She is a gorgeous dapple gray with a black and silver mane. She has nearly perfect conformation for an American Quarter Horse. Clucking, I call her over. Pricking her ears up, she prances towards me, whinnying on her way. She loves to trick ride and so do I. Stopping beside me, I slip her halter on, buckling the top shut. The small scar on her cheek, shaped like a crescent moon, reminds me of begging dad to buy her from the Mayberry Auction. I begged him to bid on her. Otherwise, she would have become glue.

"Hey baby girl, you ready to ride," I say as she muzzles the apple from my flattened palm. Scratching her forehead, I whisper, "Come on let's go," in her ear as I lead her through the gate, shutting it behind me.

Hearing the clattering of hoofs and boots behind me, I turn my head to see my sister with her horse, Silver, following her.

"Did you get lost?" I ask as she walks in sync next to me.

"No, she wouldn't come. Made me walk all the way to the far fence line to get her," she replies, frustrated with Silver's naughty behavior.

"Maybe she doesn't want to work today," I tease her.

"Oh well, she will live," she replies, showing no mercy to Silver.

"Well, you're a nice mom," I respond.

Laughing we enter the barn, hooking the horses to the cross-ties by the back room. Grabbing our grooming kits, we brush them down, making sure there are no dirt clumps to cause rubbing scars. I run the brush over Maverick's shoulders, neck, back, belly, haunches, and sides. I'm always reminded of when she was just skin and bones when I get to her sides.

"I remember when you and dad brought her home," my sister says as she brushes Silver down.

"Yeah, at least she is all plump now," I reply as I start tacking her up.

Once brushing and tacking are completed, we lead them to the outdoor arena. It's a long oval shape with stained and treated brown wood fencing. Opening the gate, we park our horses in the corner and set up the guidance markers. On the left side of the ring, a guidance fence, constructed of white stake posts and white ribbon, is set up, bending around the bottom left corner.

"You ready, sis?" she asks as we mount our steeds.

"Always," I say as I take my position. Facing Maverick towards the course, I release my outside stirrup, heading for a fender trick, the Apache. I slide my left hand up the reins, drawing her head to turn. Kicking her up with my legs, we gallop past the start of the white tape. I begin my trick after the second post, leaning towards the inside, rolling the fender around my inside thigh while sliding my outside leg over the saddle and into a straight position with my toes pointed like a ballerina. As I stretch my outside arm to the side of me and lean back, creating a straight line

23

from head to toe, I release the anxiety of telling my father into the breeze created by my galloping steed. With the end of the course coming into view, I swing my free arm and leg up and over the saddle, grabbing hold of my reins just in time to stop at the gate. Every time I do a trick a portion of my stress evaporates into the breeze. I feel like I can finally breathe again. It's my second antidote, after writing, to let my worries wash away.

"Nice one," my sister shouts as I walk back over to her.

"Thanks! Which one are you going to do?" I ask, knowing she will go for a Shoulder Stand.

"Shoulder Stand! But you probably knew that," she says as I smile at her.

"Show me what you've got then we go in and tell them," I reply as she takes off into her trick. Like always, she completes a perfect shoulder stand. Her legs are held together towards the heavens with pointed toes as she creates a straight line with her body. We continue to take turns practicing tricks for thirty more minutes before we walk out the horses. Once they are all cooled down, we untack them and take them back to the pasture.

"Ma, Dad!" my sister and I holler as we enter the house.

"What's wrong?" dad says coming around the corner to see what all the fuss is about.

"Everything alright?" mom asks as she trails behind him.

"Everything is fine. We want to talk to you," I say.

"Alright," they respond as we sit down at the kitchen table. My sister and I sit on one side of the table, while our parents sit on the other.

"I'll start," my sister says. "I don't want to go to college. I want to work at an animal rescue. I know it's not what you want me to do, but it's what I want to do with my life."

Hearing the confidence and power behind my sister's voice, my words scramble out of my mouth, "I want to write. I can't stand the business program anymore. It's making me depressed all of the time. I applied for the writing scholarship and even if I don't win, I'm going to find a way to write. I want the farm too." Exhaling I squeeze my sisters' hand, not knowing what their reactions will be.

Dad gets up, shoving the chair across the room with his legs, coldly saying "It's your life, do as you please. Just don't expect me to be here when you fall on your ass."

Slamming my fist down on the table, I stand up, knocking my chair to the floor. "Is that really what you have to say? We came to you because we thought you would understand. We're your daughters. You're supposed to support us," I say, making myself hoarse with the tears threatening to escape.

"I'm not going to support girls who won't take my advice," he shouts as he storms out, stomping his boots on the floor and slamming the front door behind him, hard enough to shake the house.

Looking down in disbelief, the tears escape, spilling over my waterline a single tear at a time.

"Girls, don't pay attention to your father. He worries about you. He just wants the best for you I promise." Ma tries to reassure us as she gets out of the chair, walking around the table to console us.

"He could at least take some interest in what we want," I stutter. I turn and run through the dining room and up the stairs. Slamming my door shut, I faceplant onto my bed, letting my grief consume me. It made my stomach drop, feeling like anything I did would never be good enough for him.

At some point through the night, my sister climbs into my bed as we shared our brokenness with each other. At least, I always know we'll have each other, no matter what happens.

Victoria Flashback

"Come back here," I holler at Alexandra as she runs away with my teddy bear.

"Catch me," she teases as she takes my bear and runs upstairs with it.

Irritated, I run after her, wanting my bear back. I named him teddy like any other little girl would do, but she likes to take him and hide him in her room. Last time I couldn't find him for a month. I wish she would knock it off.

Chapter 4

 **Decision Making**

*M*orning comes, I do not want to get out of bed. Rubbing my eyes, I roll and look at my sister. Her eyes have a rim of red around them because we spent the night crying. I thought dad might understand how it feels to be guided into a career that feels out of place for us. Grandpa wanted him to be a businessman when he was younger. I don't know if he is still mad or feels regret for pushing us as grandpa pushed him. I guess I will just have to wait and see. Shaking her shoulder softly, I awake her up.

"Hey, I was thinking after our chores are finished, we could go to Riverdale and walk through all the booths in the market," I say, reaching my hand over to push the hair out of her face. I wait a minute for a response, but she just lays there, biting the corner of her lip and staring at me. In a reassuring voice, I say, "I'm sure dad won't mind. It would be nice to have a break from everything. I don't think I can look at dad's face today for very long and keep it together."

Rolling on her back, she says, "Everything is changing really fast. Isn't it?" She grabs my teddy bear from the floor and hugs it.

"Yeah, I guess it is. They will announce the scholarship winner in only a week, and after last night, I don't think things will ever be the same." I look at her hoping she agrees. It would help both our spirits to get away for the day.

"Let's go have some fun. I'm glad it's Sunday." She grins at me, seeming to brighten up a shade.

"Sweet! Let's get it done," I say, glad I could make her feel a little better.

We throw ourselves out of bed excited for the rest of the day. I grab my favorite pair of Silver jeans hanging off the corner post of my bed and my green tank top. Throwing on my clothes, I run down the stairs and stuff my feet into my boots. Glanceing at the dinner table, I take in a deep breath and step out the door towards my chores.

It only takes us two hours to finish this morning. After we put the wheelbarrow away, we walked to the front gate, where dad is mending a fence line. We tell him where we are going; he just shrugs his shoulders and says to have fun with no emotion. He doesn't even pick up his head from his work to look at us when we ask, so we head to the house to get ready.

As I look in the mirror at my reflection, I can't help but be bothered by his words. They are just normal words that get spoken each day, but they sound different coming from his lips. They have certain malice to them as if he doesn't want to say how he really feels. Maybe with time, he will understand, but I can't wait. I have my own dreams and one day I'm going to live them.

Sighing, I loop my black leather, turquoise gemstone belt through my jeans. Once the belt is through the last, I slide the matching phone holster through it. I complete buckling my belt, being reminded of the last flea market I went to with my grandfather. There was an older gentleman there. He had his own booth with all kinds of handcrafted leather objects. I fell in love with the set as soon as I saw it.

Victoria Flashback

"Papa, can I make something, too?" I ask as I pull on his pant leg.

Pulling his eyes away from the wallet is stitching, he says, "Only if you pay attention." As he reaches down, he picks me off the wood floor of his workshop, and places me on the stool next to him. Grabbing a piece of leather, he sets it in front of me guiding my hand with the burning tool as we begin to shape a horseshoe.

"You ready?" my sister pipes in from my doorway.

"Yeah! Let's get on the road," I reply, grabbing my bag from the corner of the bedpost. Some days I wish my life wasn't so complicated. I'm always having to stay on the move. The only moments I really slow down and stop to take a breath are when I'm writing or riding. Taking a shallow breath, I follow her through the hallway and down the staircase. Sitting on the bench, we pull on our boots and walk through the front door.

"Can I drive?" she asks with her look she knows I can't say no to. That's one thing about being a big sister I will never understand. When they give you that look, you would do anything for them.

"Of course. You need to stop using that look though," I reply.

"Nahh! I'd rather not. It works all too well for me," she says.

"You are such a pain in the ass," I reply.

"Yeah, but you wouldn't know what to do without me," she laughs.

"You think you're so smart. Oh, and we're picking up Summer on the way," I inform her.

"Oh, I am. And sweet!" she exclaims.

"More like a sweet-tart! I am so good," she says.

"Keep thinking that. Let's go before daylight runs out," I say as I push her towards the doorway. She grabs my keys from the key rack as she runs to the truck. Laughing to myself, I walk after her and hop in the passenger seat of my own vehicle. "You sure you know how to drive?" I tease her.

"Shut up!" She snaps at me as the engine roars to life and we head down the driveway.

Looking out the window I can't help but think what will happen with my application. However, the sight of the fence posts going by and the cattle and horses grazing in their fields as we drive down the driveway, shooting dust and stone out the back of the tires, gives me a boost of confidence. I need to stop worrying so much and live my life the way I want to.

As we turn out of the driveway, I remember all the trouble we would get into with Summer. We grew up together, always playing in the mud and chasing each other around the ranch. She is like a sister to us. She has dirty blonde hair and sparkling blue eyes. Her smile is like a shooting star, lighting up the night sky. We would climb the haystack to the very top, try to tip the cows (the legend is extremely wrong, they charge at you instead of falling over), hide in the hayloft, and find anything we could get into trouble with. She's a good leech you can't get rid of, and we wouldn't trade her for the world.

Realizing multiple cars have passed us, I remember how slow Alexandrea drives. My sister won't go over the speed limit at all. I like to say she drives like an old granny. However, it gives me a chance to look at the scenery and check for familiar faces along the way. When I see old couples going on their Sunday drives, I like to imagine that I will find that same love one day. He doesn't have to be dashingly handsome or have a platinum card at his disposal. I just want someone who will love me for who I am. I want to be those old couples one day, going along on their Sunday drive, smiling at each other as they travel with no destination in mind.

Breaking my thoughts, the truck as it comes to a grandma-style stop. I look for Summer to come running out the front door like she always does. Sometimes I think she's going to break the door off the hinges when she comes out. Her house is two stories with yellow siding and white trim. The roof is shingled black with a front porch full of flowers. Her mom always has to have them on the porch. She has two red rose bushes, one on each side of the steps. The vines climb and wrap around the spindles of the porch railing.

The sound of the front door slamming interrupts my thoughts. "MUST YOU ALWAYS SLAM THAT DOOR SO HARD. I SWEAR YOU'RE GOING TO RIP IT OFF ITS HINGES NEXT TIME," I yell out of my window, while she charges to the truck.

"I DON'T SLAM IT," she hollers back as she opens my door and climbs into the back seat.

"Well, it's nice to see you, too," I reply. "Are you ready for the market?"

"I always am. My mother is trying to make me garden for her again. She knows I'm not a flower person. I wish she would quit," she says in annoyance.

"Welcome to the club. Dad isn't happy with us right now," Alexandrea mutters.

"What did you two do now?" she asks with her eyebrows raised.

"Would you like to tell her?" I ask, looking at my sister suggestively.

"Fine," she whines, "We told him we didn't want to do what he wants anymore and we want to do what we want."

"It didn't turn out so well," I add on.

"I'm sure you guys are stressing out for nothing. Don't dads always forgive? He forgave you when you lost his special hammer. Let's turn the radio on and listen to some music until we get there. You guys need to chill," Summer says.

"That is the plan for today," I laugh as I turn the radio on to our favorite station 94.1 Duke f.m. This is one of my favorite stations because they always play the oldies like Martina McBride, Leann Rimes, Shania Twain, and Dolly Parton. I'm pretty sure my sisters agree with me since they are singing every word at the top of their lungs, very much out of tune. Smiling, I join in on *I Was Country When Country Wasn't Cool.*

As we pull into the market, we're met by loads of people piling in and out of their cars, trucks, and SUVs. There are always a lot of people here. The booths are frequently filled with craftsmen and women, selling their handmade goods, making it my favorite market. The only difficulty is finding a place to park.

"How about we enter through the backfield?" I ask her.

"Can't we get in trouble for that?" my sister says as we continue to follow the line of cars towards the field parking entrance.

"Yeah, but they won't notice if you keep going straight and turn in at the side streets. The cars are lined up all the way down there. Besides, I've done it before and all the farm boys park down there," I assure her as she continues to drive.

"Oooh! Sounds like a great idea. I haven't gotten any action in a while," Summer squeals behind me.

"Fine, but you guys are beyond gross," Alexandrea replies with disgust as she continues straight past the entrance. As we move down the road, Summer and I look for anyone that catches our eye. There's one that I've always liked, but I don't see him here that often. He drives a red f-250 with a steel flatbed and headache rack. The front bumper is custom while the back bumper looks like a steel pole. The guy who drives it isn't that bad, either. He's around six foot five with light brown hair and blue eyes. He has a beard and a muscular, strong frame with a little bit of a belly. I never liked the appearance of a solid muscled man. Instead, I like the teddy bear effect. Sadly, I do not see him as I search through the parked vehicles.

"Alright, this is a good enough spot. Let's go," Alexandrea says as she parks the truck. We climb out and take in the vibrant green grass, the crowd of happy faces, and the chatter of things people have found as they pass us.

"That'll be two dollars per person, ladies," a sweet-looking old man smiles at us as we reach the entrance. I reach into my pocket and pull out six dollars. "Thank you, sir," I say as I hand him the money.

As we walk down the dirt path to enter the grounds, I take in the scenery. The booths are lined up in rows like grocery aisles. The vendors rent the little shed-like buildings with concrete floors. Colorful triangle-shaped flags are strung up from one rooftop to another, down each aisle, so people can see the market from afar. The buildings are made of light-colored wood and black shingled roofs. There are nearly 40 to 50 booths in the market. By the front entrance, there is a concession building with bathrooms and picnic tables. Turning, I see Summer and Alexandrea as they disappear from my view. I'm guessing they went to get food before even looking at the vendors. Chuckling, I grab a seat at one of the picnic tables.

Suddenly, I feel a tap on my shoulder. Turning my head, I catch Billy with one leg on the seat of the table and his elbow placed on it with his head cocked.

"Fancy seeing you here. You sure you still don't want to take me up on that offer?" he asks with his eyebrows raised.

"Go the hell away, Billy. You want my pistol up you're back this time," I snap at him, wanting him to leave me alone.

"You are just playing," he says in a lucrative tone as he slides around the picnic table and stands in front of me. I can feel his hot breath grow closer as he gets an inch from my face.

"Now, weren't you," he asks as he places his grubby hands on either side of me. I reach for my gun, realizing I left it at home. Seeing my mistake, he leans in closer, trying to pin me in place.

"I'm going to give you one more chance. Get off of me or you won't like what happens next," I say as I stare straight back at him with a fierce look.

"Make me," he says, pushing himself closer. I take my right leg and knee him in the groin. As he doubles over in pain, he falls backwards into the hands of the guy with the red f-250. Looking up, I'm met with the same pair of blue eyes I always look for. My breath stops as my heart beats faster. The next few moments happen in slow motion as he throws Billy into the side of the concessions building. He thuds against the brick wall.

Slowly, the handsome stranger approaches me, asking if I'm alright, but I can't speak. My heart is beating too fast. My palms are becoming sweaty as he gets closer. All I can hear is the melodic tone in his voice.

Chapter 5

A Chance Meeting

"*A*re you alright? Did he hurt you?" I ask her while she stares at me. As I walk toward her, she doesn't move. Her body looks as rigid as a light pole. Instead of rising and deflating with each breath, her chest remains at the same level. She isn't even blinking her eyes as I close the space between us.

I take my right hand and wave it in front of her face. "My name is Dustin. What's yours?" I try to break her trance. As I wait for a response, I look into her eyes. At first glance, they appear to be a light brown. However, I notice a variance in shades of brown around her irises with their flecks of amber that make them twinkle in the sunlight. Taken aback by their beauty, I realize I have seen those eyes before, but I can't remember where, her lashes accentuate her perfectly oval almond-shaped eyes. Upon further inspection, I notice her full and plump lips, beautifully.

As I continue to take in her features, I begin to see her lips start to part, revealing a set of pearly white teeth that glisten in the sunlight. Reaching my hand out, I swipe a stray hair that is covering her eyes and tuck it behind her ear.

"Yes, I ...I'm alright," she studders as she breaks her silence. She begins to look down, avoiding my eyes. I can tell she is nervous, but I don't know if it's because of me or what just happened. Her presence feels warm and inviting, causing my stomach to turn. I have never believed in love at first sight because of my childhood. But, I am unsure about the butterflies beginning to flutter in my stomach.

When I was young, my parents went through a divorce and I was constantly sent back and forth between them. Holidays were never fun because of constant car rides to see all sides of the family. Most of my friends thought it was cool to be getting more presents and having multiple Christmases or birthdays, but they didn't know the struggle behind it. I was always unhappy. I wanted to have my parents together, so I could grow up in a real family. I guess it just wasn't meant for me. I spent my night longing for that experience.

"Umm, so thanks for that. I…. I'm going to go back to my friends now," she says as she starts to walk away.

Breaking out of my trance, I rush towards her and grab her hand and ask her to "Wait!" She stops and looks at me for a minute as she raises her eyebrows in curiosity. "Could I at least get your name and walk with you until you find your friends?" I don't want her to go, taking the warmth with her. I am pretty sure those boys won't come back to harm her, but I would feel better making sure she was with her friends.

"Sure, but it's really not necessary," she smiles at me.

"Well, I would feel better making sure they don't come after you again… So, I guess you're stuck with me for now," I joke with her.

"If you say so. Last I saw my friends, they were up here. I'm guessing they got some food," Her eyes scan the grounds for them.

"Well, what do you say we start walking around and look at booths and maybe we'll run into them. They couldn't have gone far," I suggest, hoping she will agree to it.

"That sounds good. So, are you here with any friends?" She asks as we begin to walk down the row.

"No, I like to come here by myself. It gives me time to think and enjoy myself. I work a lot," I respond.

"What do you do and why do you work so much?" she asks as she places her hands in her pockets.

I pause thinking about what I want to say.

"Sorry, I'm just a curious person. I didn't mean to pry," she replies, seeming nervous.

"No, you're fine," I try to reassure her. "I have a nine-to-five job as a mechanic at my uncles' shop, but I am working on starting a business with my buddy. We are doing mobile semi repair. So, I have to be ready to go to a call any time after work or on the weekends," I try and explain to her.

"So, what happens if you get a call during the day?" she asks as she stops at the first booth and picks up a pair of Tony Llama tall, square toe black boots with turquoise stitching and embellishments.

"My buddy works third shift, so he takes care of those calls," I reply, watching her trace the stitching on the boots before she sets them back on the table.

"Oh, well it sounds like you have it all figured out. Lucky you," she replies, looking through the rest of the booth.

I continue to observe her movements as I ask, "What do you mean lucky?" I am curious about her definition of lucky.

"It sounds like things are starting to go your way. Like your dreams are beginning and life's not standing in your way," she replies, grabbing another pair of Tony Llamas.

"I guess you could say that but I'm just starting. It's not really taking off yet and there's that risk that it won't work out and fail," I reply, beginning to think there's something more to her comment.

Smiling, she looks at me for a minute. "I guess you're right. I've never thought of it like that. Guess you're smarter than you look."

"What do I look like then?" I ask her.

"Well, I could tell you like being messy. Your clothes are covered in grease and oil stains. But your strong demeanor is just a cover-up. I bet you're a big teddy bear underneath," she says with a smirk on her face.

"Wow, so I'm a big teddy bear now. Guess I just lost my rep," I laugh.

Suddenly, I hear girls hollering behind me. Turning my head, I see a blonde and brunette, jogging towards the booth.

"Hey! Where have you been?" they question her as they hook their arms through both of hers.

"I had an incident with Billy, but he helped me," she replies as she points in my direction. Turning their heads, they look at me and start to turn red with embarrassment.

"Oh! I'm sorry. We didn't even see you there," the brunette replies.

"I'm Summer and she's Alexandrea," the blonde says.

"That's alright. I'm Dustin," I tell them, not wanting my time with her not to end.

"Well, we better go. Thanks for the help again. I had fun talking to you," she replies as they turn to walk away.

"Wait! You never told me your name," I say.

Stopping for a moment, she turns her head over her shoulder and says, "It's Veronica."

As they walk away, I can't help but stare at her, moving side to side as her hips sway. She has this swing in her walk that lures me into her cute little butt bouncing with each step. Smiling, I turn back to the booth and check the price tag on the first pair of boots she picked up. The tag prices them at $200 dollars.

"Would you like to buy those?" the woman asks. "I noticed the young lady looking at them. Seems she would love these as a gift. Is she your girlfriend?"

"No, she's not," I reply not wanting to be rude.

"Well, you two looked good together and I caught the way you were smiling at her. I'll take $150 for them if you'd like," she says.

I take in the vendors' kind appearance. She looks like the fun grandma everyone would like to have with her sweet smile and bold eyes.

"I'll take them," I reply. I hand her the cash and place the boots in their box as I exit the booth.

Looking down the row, I don't see the girls anymore. It seems more time has passed than I realized since the crowds are starting to thin. I tuck the boot box under my arm and walk toward my truck. I can't help but think about her. I can't get her out of my head. There is something different about her. I feel different after being around her today. Usually, I can't shake my feelings of stress, but she brings a sense of peace I haven't felt in a long time.

As I walk through the entrance to the market, I spot my red f-250 Super Duty in the back row. There are few cars left out here anymore, so I make it to the truck within a few minutes.

Opening my door, I set the boot box on my passenger seat and place my key in the ignition as I start her up.

Chapter 6

Unknown Connection

*H*earing my engine run as I drive down the road always excites me. I love hearing the sound of the motor running and feeling the rush of power behind the steering wheel.

My phone goes interrupting my inner monologue. I reach into the center counsel and grab it. Without looking at the screen, I answer it and bring it to my ear.

"Hello," I say.

"Hey! It's dad. Could you stop and grab some buns for dinner?" he asks.

"Yeah. On my way home now," I say, ending the call.

Setting my phone down, I place my hand back on the steering wheel and continue down the streets. I have so many memories with friends here. We did a lot of things we shouldn't have. I remember racing in the night, having huge bonfires in the hay fields, and breaking into the old paper mill.

In fact, it had to of been our worst idea. We almost got trapped in there. One of my buddies, Jeff, climbed up into one of the lofts. We told him not to because the floorboards were worn and creaking. He wouldn't listen to us and kept saying we were just worrying too much, but when he got up to the top the boards gave out. We heard a loud snap and before we knew it, he was laying on the ground in a pile of broken boards. The patrol officer, Bruce, was parked across the street. We heard him flip his sirens on, thinking he was coming for us. Luckily, he was going after a speeding, drunk driver. I had to grab my buddy and carry him out of the mill as we ran out. Fortunately, he just got the wind knocked out of him. However, I never felt more scared after that night.

My outlook on life changed after the paper mill. I stopped drinking every night, chewing tobacco, and I became more focused on my future. Seeing Jeff nearly lose his life over one split-second decision made me realize how fragile life can be. I learned how fast it can be taken away with no warning. This is the moment that changed me and taught me a lesson I'll never forget or take for granted.

As I turn onto Groover St., the corner store comes into view. I pull over into a parking spot and put my truck in park. Luckily, no one is parked here, so I don't have to parallel park my truck. The spaces are already small enough, so it's not easy to fit my big-ass truck in these spots.

Climbing out, I grab my phone out of the center counsel and place it in my back pocket. I take my keys out of the ignition and hook them to my belt loop. As I reach the front doors, I notice an old couple coming up behind me. I tip my ball cap and say hello as I hold the door open for them.

"Thank you, young man," the old woman smiles at me as she and her husband walk through the door.

"You're welcome," I say, not thinking anything of my actions. I always do this for people. I was raised to have manners and to be a gentleman.

I walk into the store behind the couple and let the door wing shut behind me, causing the bell to ring. The owner looks up at us from the register and smiles. Any time I come in here, he is always happy to see his customers.

Returning his smile, I walk to the middle isle and grab a pack of stadium buns off the shelf. Looking over the top of the shelf, I notice the old couple picking out their ice cream flavors. They look like teenagers again when they look at each other. I can still see the love and infatuation in their eyes. I can hear the women giggle as her husband makes a joke about the moose track flavor. She reminds me of an older Veronica with her big smile and mesmerizing eyes.

Shaking my head, I go to the register and grab two Reese's bars. It's my favorite candy bar.

"Is that all for you?" the owner asks as he rings up the buns and candy bar.

"I need a pack of Marlboro Menthol Gold Shorts too," I reply, knowing this is another habit I should break. He grabs the pack of cigarettes off the back wall and rings them up.

"That will be $12.30, please."

I hand him a five and a ten and tell him to keep the change. It's just a couple of dollars. I don't need it. "Have a nice night," I say as I exit the store.

Unhooking my keys from my belt loop, I open my driver's door and climb into the seat. I set the buns on top of the boot box, open the center counsel, set my smokes in it, and open my candy bar.

As I drive towards my house, I blast my stereo and listen to Nickle Back, *Far Away*.

I live with my father on Mayberry Street. He is a retired mechanic and can no longer work in shop because of his shoulders and knees. He recently had surgery on his right shoulder, but it hurts him even more now. Some of my best memories are working on cars with him.

Turning my headlights off, I grab the buns and boot box. I hit the garage door opener on my visor before I shut my front door. The garage is cluttered with tools and boat motors. It's his only source of income, since he can't work in a shop anymore.

I can hear him call the dogs back as I hit the garage door opener on the wall and walk into the house. I set the buns on the counter and walk to the living room with the boot box. The house needs some work. There are holes in all the walls. At one time, there was a rat infestation, so the exterminators had to fumigate the house and set a bunch of traps in the walls. All the dry wall needs replaced, the hardwood floor needs refinished, the cabinets and trim need to be replaced, and it needs a serious deep clean. But, it's still livable, so I don't care. In my opinion it's a roof over my head for now. One day, I will have a house of my own in much better condition.

"So, did you have fun?" my dad asks as I set down in the brown recliner, placing the boot box on my lap.

"Yeah, it was nice," I reply, not sure if I should tell him about meeting Veronica.

"Sounds like it was more than just nice," he says as he lifts his eyes up from his phone and looks at me.

Meeting his gaze, I take a deep breath in and tell him about Veronica.

I tell him of Billy and how he harassed her. When I finish, he asks if the boots are for her.

"Yeah, they are. She was looking at them when we were in the booth. She kept saying how she always wanted a pair of Tony Llamas. The women in the booth gave me a deal on them because of the way I was looking at her," I say.

"It sounds like there is something else you want to say," he says, continuing to look at me.

For a moment I look him in the eyes and think about my mother and him. I have always wondered if maybe love, at first sight, could be real, but I've always doubted it because of their relationship.

"Does it have to do with our divorce?" he asks still searching for an answer.

I take a deep breath in and say "Well, I've never believed in love because of you and mom, but I couldn't help feel something different being around Veronica today. I just felt like I have known her forever. Like she isn't a stranger," I reply, looking back down at the boots.

"Son, just because me and your mom didn't work out. It doesn't mean your relationship will be like that. I know our split was tough for you and it wasn't always fun going back and forth. I am sorry for that. I wish we could have given you the childhood you always wanted but you have to remember. You can't keep letting the past influence your decisions today. You have to take a chance sometimes and you might be surprised on the outcome," he says as he leans back into his chair.

"Thanks, dad! I didn't hate my childhood. I just wanted to know what it felt like to be a family," I reply not wanting him to feel bad.

"So, what did you say her name was again?" he asks.

"Veronica."

"And was the boy bothering her named Billy.? Isn't he one of Sheriff Thomas's boys that terrorizes the town?" he asks.

"Yeah," I reply confused.

"I believe her full name is Veronica Salyer. She works at Mamma's Place in town," he says.

"How do you know that?" I ask.

"I am friends with one of the regulars, Tootsie, there. She talks about her all the time. Her father is a big name in town, too. You will have to treat her right. He is very protective, especially after what happened with Billy," he says.

"What do you mean after what happened with Billy? You have to tell me," I insist, needing to know everything now. I couldn't help but feel a sense of anger wash over me as he started describing Billy's obsession with her.

For the next couple of hours, we talked about Veronica and her incident with Billy while I struggled to keep my knuckles from turning white as I gripped the arm of the chair. It was midnight before my head was able to hit my pillows.

Chapter 7

 New Beginnings

*G*rabbing my bedroom door handle, I open my door quietly, so I don't wake my parents from the creaking. Summer and Alexandrea follow in behind me. Sighing, I set my bag down on my bed. I bought a few things on the way out of the market. As we left, there was another booth with lots of leatherwork. I saw a hand-tooled black and turquoise belt with a silver buckle and rhinestones. While I was looking at that belt, the sun hit an emerald green gem on another belt, causing it to shimmer. I bought that belt too.

"So, did you like Dustin?" Summers asks me as she sits in my computer chair, spinning in place.

"Yeah. I would have been able to handle Billy though, but I think he is the guy who drives the f-250 that I always look for. I've only seen him a handful of times before this, but he looked so familiar to me." I grab one of my pillows and hug it to my chest.

"Well, you got to meet your dream man then," my sister says as she sits on the other end of my bed. "Did you get his number?"

Stuffing my head into the pillow, I reply, "No, we just exchanged names. I do know he works as a mechanic though."

"Did he say what shop?" Summer asks.

"No."

"Have you checked the scholarship competition?" Summer asks.

"They will send a letter in the mail when they decide and I'm worried I won't win," I reply not wanting to think about it. Sighing, I shove my face into my pillow more, trying to find some peace in my thoughts. Everything has happened so fast today that I can't think straight. Dad is still upset and doesn't seem like he is going to be talking to us anytime soon.

"Hey, everything will be alright," Summer and my sister say as they sit on either side of me, causing my mattress to sink.

For the rest of the night, we sit there and reminisce about old memories. At some point, the three of us fall asleep on my bed.

Fathers POV

Sitting in my chair, I can't help but think about the words my daughters spoke to me. I've never tried or wanted to hold them back from their dreams. I just want them to do better than I did when I started out. I went through the struggle of taking on my father's business. It wasn't easy to keep up with his legacy.

In the beginning, I was always scared I would screw up and ruin everything he worked for. I was constantly worried and stressed out. I worked myself to the point of exhaustion because I worried about what other people would think. Was I doing as good of a job as he did? Was I making him proud? I don't want my daughters to have the same worry.

"Honey, are you alright," I hear my wife ask as she walks through the living room and sits on my lap.

Holding onto her and burying my head in her chest, I lean the recliner back and take in her sweet scent. It always calms me down when I am worried.

"Are you still worried about the girls?" she asks as she runs her fingers through my tousled hair.

"Yeah, I just don't understand why they can't see what I am trying to do for them," I reply as I hug her closer to me.

Chuckling, she places her hands on either side of my face and brings my lips to hers. For a moment we exchange a kiss of comfort and reassurance that causes my body to melt into her touch. "They do understand," she replies as she lifts her lips from mine and continues to look into my eyes.

"They just need some time. You are going to have to realize that their dreams aren't going to be the same as yours. I know you're stubborn like you're Gma was, but you will have to let them decide for themselves. You can't always protect them," she says.

Placing my hand on her cheek and tracing my thumb over her lips, I reply "How did I get so lucky to have such a wise and beautiful wife?"

Smiling, she kisses my forehead before getting off my lap. "How about we go upstairs and have some time of our own. The girls went out tonight with Summer. We have the house to ourselves tonight," she suggests.

I get up off my chair and grab her hand as she leads me up the staircase to our room. I was hoping to try and talk to them again, but I understand if they need their space. Looking at my wife's back, I appreciate her slender form, long wavy hair, and plump bottom. No matter how long we've been together, I still get lost in her beauty. She keeps me on earth.

Waking up to the sun peeking through my curtains, I check my phone to see what time it is. The screen lights up to read nine a.m. "Shit," I almost shout, knowing I am running late for my shift. I am usually up early to help with chores before work, but I must have overslept this time.

"What's going on?" Summer and my sister grumble in unison as I try to get off the bed without hitting them.

"I am running late," I reply hurriedly as I grab the first pair of jeans I see.

"Don't worry, I'll help today just get to work," Summer grumbles as she pushes my sister into a sitting position.

"Thanks, You're the best," I whisper as I grab my new turquoise belt, work t-shirt, and phone. Shutting the door behind me, I run to the bathroom, throw my clothes on, brush my teeth, and throw my hair into a messy bun.

As I run down the staircase, I can hear my mom holler from the kitchen about breakfast. However, I'm running too late, so I slide my boots on and run to my truck. Grabbing my driver's door handle, I slide into my seat and start my engine. As I pull out of the drive, I leave a cloud of dust trailing behind me.

I hope Mrs. Kay doesn't get mad at me. I am never late to a shift. As I drive down the road, I can't help, but let my mind drift to Dustin. When

I was with him, I felt relaxed for the first time in a while. It's like he took the stress away from me and made everything seem alright. I hope I run into him again.

Smiling to myself, I turn into the parking lot and park in my spot. I grab my apron off my back seat and run into the restaurant. Mrs. Kay can hear the bells jingle as I open the door.

"You're late," she says as she walks over to me after pouring coffee for a table.

"I know, I am so sorry. Summer came over last night and I overslept," I say hoping she'll forgive me.

She hands me the coffee pot and says "I am just messing with you. Get to work honey" as she goes to greet another table.

Laughing to myself at her sarcasm failure, I take the coffee pot and put it back on the burner before tying my apron around my waist. Turning around, I start greeting the regulars at the counter. They all get their usual orders, so I ring them in and get their drinks.

As the morning goes on, Mrs. Kay and I serve the customers, while talking about her recent visit with her grandchildren. Her kids grew up and moved away from here to Montana, but they still visit once a year so she can see her grandkids. Mrs. Kay lives for those visits. Sometimes I think she would like them to move back here, but she pretends she doesn't miss them that much.

"Could I get a cup of coffee?" I hear a male voice ask me as I am grabbing an order from the window.

"After I deliver this food," I say as I take the food to its table.

Grabbing a coffee cup, I pace it in front of the voice, realizing its Dustin. "What are you doing here?" I am surprised because I've never seen him here and didn't tell him where I worked yesterday.

"I had to see you again and my dad knows your family," he sayss as I pour the coffee into his cup.

Setting the pot back in its place, I grab the creamer and sugar to place in front of him.

"That's alright, I like it black," he says as he brings the cup to his lips.

I can't help but stare at his features as he drinks his coffee. He has stormy blue eyes I can get lost in. His hair is curly and his jawline is strong and pronounced. But, his lips, full and plump, beg to be kissed.

"So, is it a good surprise?" he asks as he sets his cup down.

"Ummm... Yeah. Sorry, I zoned out for a minute," I say, feeling my cheeks heating up.

"It's alright. I just wanted to see if you would like to go out with me sometime?" he asks as he finishes his cup.

"When were you thinking?" I ask, leaning on the counter with my arms crossed not realizing how close I'm leaning into him.

"How about Friday night? I'll pick you up at seven for a movie and dinner," he says with a twinkle in his eye.

Feeling excited, I reply "that sounds great." Grabbing a pen and paper out of my apron, I write down my number and address. I hand him the piece of paper and lean back off the counter.

He puts the paper in his pocket and gets up from the stool. As he walks out, he stops at the door and takes one last glance in my direction before leaving the restaurant.

Smiling, I continue to finish my shift while being completely distracted by thoughts of him and anticipation of our date.

Chapter 8

 ***Past to Present***

*A*s the week moves on, I continue to think about Friday night. I can't wait to go out with him. However, I'm curious as to how his dad knows my family. I have never heard anyone in my family say his name before. I can't help but wonder if that's why he seems so familiar to me.

"Hey, you ready to ride?" my sister asks as she opens my bedroom door.

"Yeah, I can't believe my date is tomorrow night. The week has gone by so fast," I say, grabbing my backpack off my bedpost.

"That's because you have been daydreaming all week," she teases me as we walk down the staircase to the front door.

"I can't help it. He said his dad knew our family and I'm really curious about how," I reply, still trying to figure it out how in my head.

"Why don't you ask dad tonight? Maybe he will tell you," she says as we get into my truck to drive to school.

"I can try. Still not sure if he is talking to us," I reply as I blast the stereo and drive down the lane.

The bell sounds, signaling the end of school. Grabbing my books off my desk, I place them back into my bag.

"Veronica," Mrs. Wilder calls me as I go to exit the classroom. Turning around, I walk over to her desk.

"Yes ma'am," I reply, wanting to leave.

"I wanted to let you know that I would love to write a letter of recommendation for you. There is this amazing scholarship going on for your program. Just let me know. I would be more than happy too," she says as she hands me a printout of the scholarship.

Taking the pamphlet from her, I thank her and walk out of the classroom. I feel the pressure begin to build on me again. I just wish she and my father would stop pushing me into this program. On my way to the front doors, I throw the pamphlet into the nearest recycling bin.

"Hey! Could I get your notes again? Promise I will give them back tomorrow," Sky asks me.

"Yeah, here you go," I hand them to her as I pull them out of my bag.

"Thanks! You're a lifesaver. My car went into the shop today so my parents dropped me off," she replies as she stuffs the notes into her bag.

"Is that why you missed class this morning?"

"Yeah, and I love taking a look at Dustin. He's one of the mechanics there," she says with googly eyes as we walk towards the front doors.

"Blonde hair and blue eyes drive a red f-250?" I ask curious if it's the same Dustin I have a date with.

"Yep, that's him. How'd you know?" she asks with a perplexed expression.

"I met him at the flea market. He came into work and asked me out Friday," I say as I open the front doors. "By the way, what's his last name?"

"Shaw. You're a lucky girl. See ya tomorrow!" she exclaims as she hops into her father's SUV.

Smiling to myself, I hop in my truck and head home to ask my dad.

"Dad," I holler as I walk into the front door. I didn't see him in the fields and his truck is still here. I walk from the living room to the kitchen, trying to find him.

"I'm in my office," he says as I walk past his doorway.

"Hey, I know we haven't talked since last time, but I have an important question for you," I say hoping he will talk to me.

"Okay, what is it?" he asks in an annoyed tone as he looks up from his books.

Pulling the chair out from in front of his desk, I sit in and ask him if he knows Dustin Shaw's family. He tells me of a feud between his family and mine. Apparently, our grandfathers were friends, but they got into a disagreement over land. Dustin's grandfather did all the repairs on the farm equipment. One day the bailer decided to break. It started sputtering and smoking in the field. According to my grandfather, he rigged the bailer instead of fixing it. They argued over who was right and ended up not speaking to each other. Since then, our fathers were never allowed to play together again.

As my dad told the story, I couldn't help but feel shocked at the history. I always thought my grandfather got along with everyone.

"Why does Dustin seem familiar to me?" I ask him.

Leaning back in his chair, he replies, "You were young when we last saw them. We had gone into the corner store. You and Dustin started looking through the candy together. I grabbed you and pulled you away. For the rest of that night, you cried because I took you away from your new friend," he replies, looking down into his lap.

Shaking my head, I stand up, sending the chair backwards into the wall. "So, you dragged your young daughter away from a friend because you had to make grandpa's grudge yours," I yell in disbelief.

"I'm sorry Veronica, but your grandfather was right. He did rig our equipment," he sternly says as he gets out of his chair to walk toward me.

Not wanting to hear any more from my father, I run out of the house and started doing my chores.

The next day goes as usual. I do my chores, go to class, do some more chores, and get ready for my date. My father still doesn't know I am going out with Dustin, but I don't care what he thinks. What happened between our grandfathers has nothing to do with us. I look in the mirror at my reflection. I am in my favorite pair of wranglers, my new turquoise belt, gray tank top, and a turquoise flannel shirt. I decide to leave my hair down and let it blow in the wind. I have a weird sense of self-confidence starting to grow inside me.

"Hey, I got some mail for you," Alexandrea says as she enters my room excitedly.

Grabbing the pile form from her, I see the envelope from the New Haven School of Composition. "It's here!" I exclaim as I sit on the edge of my bed. Carefully, I open it and pull out the paper. Closing my eyes, I take in one last deep breath before I read it. As I exhale and unfold the letter, I open my eyes and begin to read.

Epilogue

I peer up from my notebook to see the bulletin board filled with pictures of Veronica. I can't get her out of my head. When I walk past her in the hallways, the smell of her lavender-scented shampoo entices me. I track her every movement like a shadow. The red lines follow her extracurricular activities. The green lines show the people who are close to her, and the white lines demonstrate her work schedule.

I look down and write:

Eyes that beam, eyes that glisten, the spotlight that contends becomes an in-transit of love. Lavender, a curer of inflammation, reverses its properties. The longer I'm kept away from her, the more my emotions become atomic. Years past to present can't contend with the emergence of emotions that boil at the mere glimpse of you. The longer I'm kept waiting for the return of emotions, the more my heart stirs.

My feverish writing comes to an end as I place my pen in its holder. I grab a pushpin out of a container and pin my poem to Veronica next to a picture of her performing at the last county fair before her grandfather passed.

"Are you coming?" my father asks as he walks toward my bedroom.

I get out of my chair and quickly close my secret door in my closet before he comes into my room.

I hear my door open as I begin to rifle through shirts to wear tonight.

"Bud, are you going to answer me?"

"Yeah, I'm just changing," I say as he walks in and sits at the foot of my bed.

"I know it's a tuff night, but I really appreciate you and your brothers supporting me. Lucy may not be your mother, but she is a nice person and cares for you," he says as he looks down at his knees.

"I know, dad. She just can't replace mom though." I grab a gray flannel shirt and button it up after I close the closet door behind me.

"I'm sorry, son. I should have taken her into an emergency sooner. Maybe I could have saved her. I'll never forgive myself for that, but I hope you and your brothers can someday," he says as he walks out of my room.

I don't say anything. I've never been able to since that night. Mom was everything to us. She always made things better when he was too drunk to function. He would stumble through the door and come after us, but she was there to stop him. I never understood why she stayed with him, but his alcohol addiction led to her death.

I feel tears escape my eyes as I grab my keys and head downstairs. Lucy and my father are waiting for me at the marble kitchen counter. They are laughing and acting like they are already married. I feel anger well up inside me as I watch them. Lucy shouldn't be here. It should be my mother, cooking dinner for us like she always did.

"Son, come say hi to Lucy," my dad says.

"Hi," I say as I grab my coat off the hook. "I'll meet you at the restaurant. I have to stop and do something first"

"Do you know what restaurant?" he asks.

"Olive Garden on 4th St. at eight." I open the door and get in my car.

Sometimes, I think my father forgets I grew up without him. I didn't need him then, so why do I need him now. He will never be the father I wanted him to be.

As I round street corners, I listen to the memories of my mother playing like a movie reel. She may be gone, but I can still feel her presence when I'm driving. My Camaro was hers.

Unknown POV Flashback

"Do you want ice cream or the hot dog stand?" Mom turns on the ignition and pulls out of the driveway as she looks through the rearview mirror at us.

"ICE CREAM," we say, knowing she is trying to make us forget about father's episode.

I can see her green eyes surrounded by black and blue bruises through her makeup. She tells stories to the towns folk to cover up father's beatings. They believe she is just clumsy and hurts herself, but we know the truth. Her eyes are filled with hurt as she drums her cut-up fingers on the steering wheel. He promises her it will be the last time after he sobers up the next morning, but it's all lies. He never changes and he never will.

Printed in the United States
by Baker & Taylor Publisher Services